Sassparilla's New Shoes

Written by Ming and Wah

Illustrated by Mariko and Adam

E.M. Press, Inc.
Manassas, VA

SASSPARILLA'S NEW SHOES
Written by Deming Chen and Dehua Chen
Illustrated by Mariko Jesse and Adam Bartley

ISBN: 1-880664-26-7
Library of Congress Catalog Card Number: 98-49701

Inquiries should be addressed to:

E.M. Press
P.O. Box 4057
Manassas, Virginia 20108

For our Ah Ping Jie, Chan Sau-Yung
Ming & Wah

For Mum and Dad
Mariko

For my sister Natasha
Adam

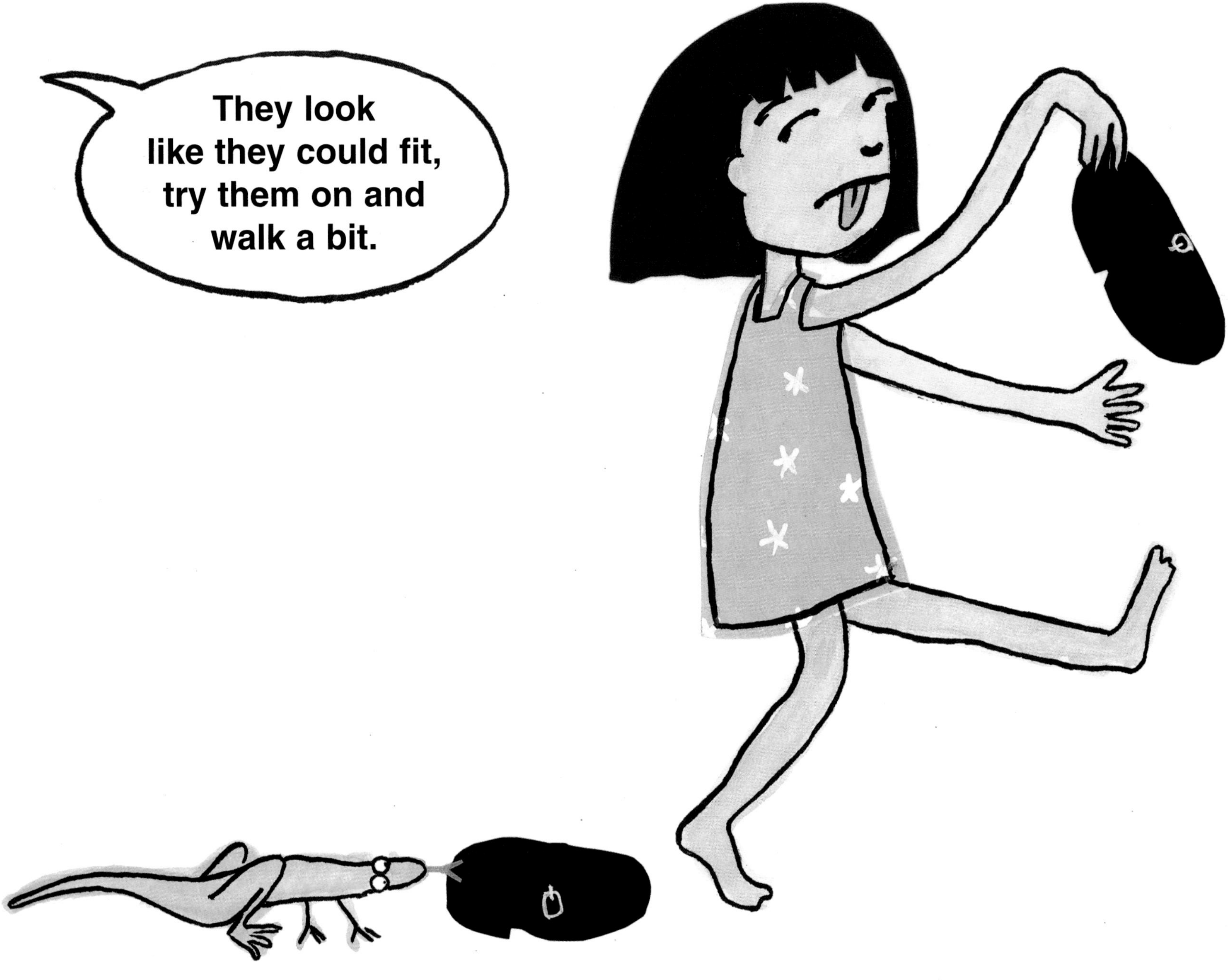
They look like they could fit, try them on and walk a bit.

"But Manuella always gets them new,

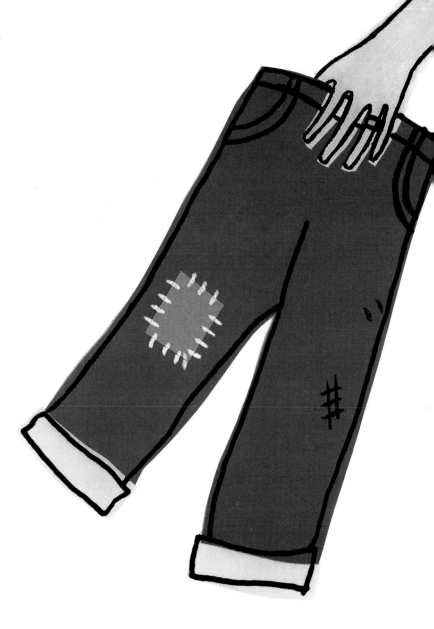

I only get them when she's through."

"And everything I've ever owned,

I've never ever owned alone!"

"I think if I could choose,
I would want these kinds of shoes:"

MOONBOOTS for the deep white snow,

GLASS SLIPPERS to make me glow.

PLATFORM SHOES to dance all day,

GALOSHES, too, to splash and play.

GENIE SHOES so I can fly,

KARATE SHOES to kick the sky.

TAP DANCING SHOES that go click-clop,

CLIMBING BOOTS to reach the top.

COWBOY BOOTS to keep the peace,

GETA SHOES like in the East.

CLOGS to stomp and clomp about,

FLIPPERS for when I get wet.

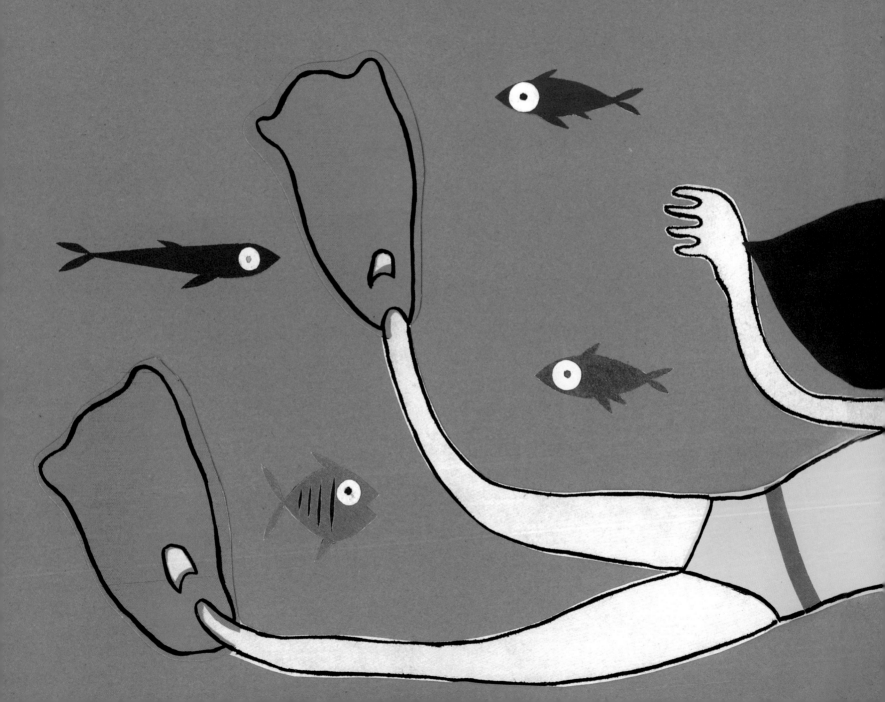

BALLET SLIPPERS to pirouette.

SOCCER CLEATS to help me win,

SKATES to twirl and whirl and spin.

"No, no, Mama! Take them back!
Manuella's shoes are from the rack."

"I simply will not be seen in such plain maryjanes,
If I have to wear them, they'll have to change."

Sassparilla scratched her head, wrinkled her nose, and assumed her serious thinking pose.

"I will paint them purple, green and red,
and line them, too, with sleek satin thread."

"I will lace them with long stems of flowers,
and give them special Sassparilla powers."

"These shoes will take me to

a place where all things old are new."

"Where everyone will stop and stare

and desperately will want a pair."

"But these shoes will be one of a kind

because I have made them truly mine."

End...